CHINESE WHISPERS

A HUTCHINSON NOVELLA

General Editor: Frank Delaney

MAURICE LEITCH

·CHINESE WHISPERS·

WITH ILLUSTRATIONS BY
SAM HUNTER

HUTCHINSON

LONDON   MELBOURNE   AUCKLAND   JOHANNESBURG

Series Design by Craig Dodd

First published in 1987 by Hutchinson, an imprint of
Century Hutchinson Ltd, Brookmount House, 62–65 Chandos Place,
London WC2N 4NW

Century Hutchinson Australia Pty Ltd
PO Box 496, 16–22 Church Street, Hawthorn, Victoria 3122, Australia

Century Hutchinson Group New Zealand Ltd
PO Box 40–086, Glenfield, Auckland 10, New Zealand

Century Hutchinson Group South Africa (Pty) Ltd
PO Box 337, Bergvlei 2012, South Africa

Leitch, Maurice
Chinese whispers. – (Hutchinson novellas).
I. Title
823'.914[F]   PR6062.E46

ISBN 0 09 172727 8

Typeset in Monophoto Photina by
Vision Typesetting, Manchester

Printed in Great Britain by
Butler & Tanner Ltd, Frome and London

A HUTCHINSON NOVELLA

BY THE SAME AUTHOR

The Liberty Lad
Poor Lazarus
Stamping Ground
Silver's City

CHINESE WHISPERS

ONE

Taking me aside one morning, Dr Beck said, 'Kenny,' in his soft voice, 'Kenny, I have a new recruit for your little circle.'

He's a small, bald, nut-brown man without trace of accent, yet he's definitely not English or one of us, although the phone book has a column and a half of Becks. Dr Verner Beck. Not quite right, somehow. He had his hand on the sleeve of my white coat as he steered me through one of the plastic flapping doors that divide the corridors here.

'I know you will do everything in your power to make him feel at home. Gavin will need time to adjust, though. He has been in Willis for the past four years.' Willis Wing is on the top floor: it's for the rich and solitary. They have their own bathrooms, even TVs, up there.

'Just between the two of us, Kenny, I want you to keep an eye out for him. It would be tragic if regression were to set in, after all the effort and time we've given to his case.'

We continued to stroll in silence, just like two colleagues on equal professional footing, only I knew and he knew the truth of the matter. His white coat, although standard issue like everyone else's, always seemed to have a superior crispness and fit, but then that may well be me and my fancies. I'm all too aware of my failings in that respect.

At the end of the corridor we went our separate ways, he to his office overlooking what was once the lake and is now the sunken rose garden after last year's mishap with that woman in Ward Six, and me to my first little performance of the day. Oh dear, the games some of us have to play . . .

Taking my shoes off outside the basement toilet, I gently ease open the heavy, scarred door. Now I'm standing on those chill tiles holding my breath. It's the coldest place in the entire building, a permanent ice-box even at the height of summer. I look, I listen, frozen there. I glance at the third cubicle from the right, in particular. It's the only one that's occupied. Surprise, surprise. I go down with one palm flat on the clammy floor until I can see underneath, but no planted feet. Again, surprise, surprise. I creep across the floor to the adjacent stall and, with practised care, mount pedestal and bowl. I look over the partition. Crouched on the throne below is Fergus Tate, a hand stuffed in his mouth to hold back the giggles, bright eyes fixed on the back of the door. I dismount, go out into the middle of the floor and cough loudly.

'Oh, dear, oh, dear,' I hear my voice ring out. 'Wherever can Fergus be? I've searched high and I've searched low. But if he's nowhere to be found, what are we going to do?'

I wait then. The damp cold is rising through my stocking-feet and I ask myself why do I persist with this foolishness . . . why?

'Ah, but, my dear Kenny,' I can hear Dr Beck's silken tones. 'What may appear make-believe outside these walls can and, quite often, does have a totally different implication for us in *our* little world.' Well, okay, doc, if you say so . . .

I stand there waiting for Fergus to reveal himself. Sometimes it can take as long as five minutes but today I'm not in a mood to prolong things so I clear my throat a second time and announce, 'Ah, well, it certainly looks as if he's not in here,' making my way across the floor as noisily as is possible in the circumstances.

2   This has the desired effect, for the cubicle door swings open.

Fergus looks out at me from his perch with hurt in his eyes. I pretend surprise. 'Goodness me!' Fergus giggles then, and drops to the floor. I hold out my hand and he runs towards me like a happy child. This is always a tricky moment; I fear for my unprotected feet. For, the fact of the matter is, Fergus is a man in his middle fifties and on the heavy side.

We went upstairs then, hand in hand, and it was like hauling a heavy, unresponsive weight. Most of his energy had gone into the game and, like any infant now, all he wanted was a nap.

After I had settled him with the rest of the group in the recreation room upstairs I took a turn along the corridors for want of nothing better to do. In this line of work you find yourself savouring such tiny escapes, so I wandered with my thoughts past the rows of high windows that overlook the grounds. You can still make out the sockets in the frames where the bars used to be.

Sometimes I wonder what must it have been like in those early days. A lot of fear, noise too, probably, for I have a sudden clear picture of faces and hands gripping those bars, trying to shake them. That's changed now, of course. We're taught to look *in*, not *out*, any more. The real world being in here, not out there, in a manner of speaking.

I must say I enjoy these moments to myself, but then something happened that was to take away most of the pleasure. As I was passing one of the doors on the right of me, it suddenly swung open. I was startled because, on this particular floor at least, they are supposed to be kept locked at all times. Someone called, 'Ssst! Ssst!' and it was Nurse Dobbs, grinning out at me, his ugly red face outlined against a background of folded linen. He crooked a finger and, although I've never had much time for him or his type, I allowed myself to be pulled into the tiny storeroom, for that's what it was.

'I've something to show you,' he said, leaning close so that I   3 could smell the cigarette reek that never leaves him. With horror, I thought of the consequences of a carelessly discarded butt in a place like this.

'Something tasty.'

Dropping to the floor, he prised apart two of the bottom pairs of laundered sheets and pulled out a magazine of some sort. When I saw the cover, a naked woman bending over the open bonnet of a car with her legs apart, I knew what was inside, all that pink, glistening meat in close-up. I tried to pull away but he held my arm in a tight grip and said, 'No, no, this is *nothing*. Have a look at *these*. See if you recognise anybody.'

From the middle of the magazine he produced a wad of photographs, the sort you take yourself, the instant variety, in colour, and offered them to me. No, he actually put them into my hand, so I had to look at them. What else could I do? I've seen him punch patients on his bad days and I don't want to make an enemy of someone like that. The poses were all of the same woman, young, brunette and, of course, naked on a bed – lying, crouched, the usual variations. I mean, everyone has seen such pictures, even children.

'Well? *Well?*'

Dobbs, I could see, was excited in more ways than one.

'Look at them again!'

I was beginning to feel desperate because the woman's face meant nothing to me. Then I began to examine the rest of the photograph and had a strange sensation, for the room – what I could see of it – did seem familiar, and in a disturbing way. The bed, for instance, white-painted metal, and that Dutch windmill pattern on a piece of curtain. And the edge of a locker, also metal, but highly polished, the sort you see in hospitals.

'My God,' I said. 'These were taken *here*!'

Dobbs laughed heartily. 'Trust you to notice *that*. First.'

4 I looked at the woman's face again. The eyes stared at the

camera with those tell-tale pinpoints of colour that you get with a flash, but there was a hungry glitter there that had nothing to do with the light.

'Maybe you don't recognise her without her clothes.'

I shuffled the photographs once more, really, just to please him, for I still couldn't place the eyes or the mouth, the hair cut short like a boy's: the rest meant nothing to me, naturally.

'It's Natalie, dope. Natalie in one—o—two.'

There *was* a girl by that name. I'd seen her walking out of doors in all weathers with her head lowered to the ground as if searching for something. She had a limp too, I remembered. That, in some strange way, only seemed to make it worse.

'Not bad, you've got to admit. Pity to waste it, eh?' He nudged me with his free hand and I moved as far away from him as I could in that small space. It was stifling in there.

'Look,' I said, 'you don't know what harm you might be doing. To her, I mean.'

His face changed and he bent to put the photographs carefully back inside their hiding-place. 'She's like a rabbit, I tell you. Can't get enough of it.'

I could see a bald spot on the crown of his head. It was the size of an egg and, somehow, looked just as fragile. It seemed the perfect target, if I'd wanted one. We all have thoughts like that, I suppose, only most of us don't do anything about them.

Then he looked up at me with a grin on his face. 'Understand? But, no, I don't suppose you would, would you, Kenny, *darling?*'

I felt for the door handle behind me with sweating palms as he rose. 'Don't despair, though. Little bird tells me you're about to have a nice new playmate of your very own. Just your type.'

Then he grabbed me low and hard with cruel force. 'You're welcome to the Polaroid any time. Just say the word.'

I smelt his tobacco breath and could have counted every pore on his face – if I'd wanted to. We seemed to be fixed in the position,   5 then, despite the pain, I pushed him away. He only laughed as he fell back against the linen. 'Hasn't Herr Doktor told you yet? It's our celebrity from upstairs. The Man in Room Forty-Two.'

I managed to make my way out of the store room and closed the door behind me. In the corridor I was sure I could hear the sound of his laugh follow me, even though I knew he was still shut up back there. I felt like putting my hands over my ears to blot it out but then had a picture of myself no different from those patients I'd seen. It was something they did, as well, to keep the world at bay. There were tears in my eyes, tears of humiliation. I went back downstairs feeling the day had been ruined.

TWO

The second floor recreation room is much nicer than its name might indicate. In fact, it's large and airy and quite pleasantly decorated, with modern windows overlooking the lawns and borders. There are easy chairs, coffee-tables, a piano (of which I have the key) and, of course, high on the wall, a twenty-three-inch television set. The pictures are of the usual restful variety, landscapes mostly, with a lot of sky and moving cloud, and the carpet is a shade of moss green, which happens also to be the dominant hue in the pictures. It often reminds me of the residents' lounge in a better-class seaside hotel. And, at first glance, the people sitting there could almost be taken for the guests you might see in such places. But then, as you get closer, certain characteristics assert themselves, certain differences. Around the walls you would notice at least a dozen or so either asleep or nodding off in dressing-gowns, but not all of them old or senile, by any means. This outer ring stays much the same; they each have their own armchair, but if ever someone curls up in someone else's nest by accident, there's never any real fuss, just a tiny, muffled commotion soon settled. I call them 'the hibernators', even though they do tend not to distinguish between the seasons.

The next ring of my charges are a little livelier: most dress in their ordinary clothes. Their chairs are not so yielding and few

insist on proprietorial rights. They glance at the television now and again or push pieces around on a draughts board.

Next we come to the centre of the room where my own little group have their territory. I sometimes think, fancifully, perhaps, that this room is like a pool and any turbulence always starts here. By the time the ripples lap the outer walls the sleepers there are rocked gently, nothing more.

Today George is standing by his chair dialling imaginary numbers in the air, but then perhaps they are real: no one has ever been able to discover. I say, 'Getting through all right, George?' He shakes his head and continues with the long distance calls that have never reached anyone at the other end.

Sometimes when the mood is on us, and it can and does happen, someone will tap on imaginary glass and tell him to get a move on, can't he see there's a queue waiting? A strange expression comes over his face at such times; you can see him hesitate, then he surrenders his place and waits patiently until the others have tired of the game. I don't really know how this sort of thing all began, perhaps some wet afternoon – there's a lot of them in this part of Ireland – when the outer ring of sleepers seemed even more deadened than usual. Many of the livelier ones resent being encircled by these reminders of what drugs and depression can do to them. They recognise that the distance between themselves and the rest is a short one to travel, in every sense. That's all a bit deep, I suppose. Dr Beck would be able to explain it much better than I could ever hope to do. Anyway, facts are facts, and all of them do have the knack of drawing attention to themselves.

Today only George was on his feet, forefinger drilling holes in the air as usual, the rest sprawled in their chairs. They had a restless look about them, as though waiting for something to happen.

'Hello, everyone,' I said. 'Hello, Connie, Harold, Lyle, Fergus, Declan, Stella.'

'Is it true, or is it not,' demanded Stella, 'that there's going to be no Christmas panto this year? Harold says we're to have a carol service instead.'

Stella – or Steve, as he used to be known – was knitting something in pink angora. The needles flashed angrily and his stubbled jowls were flushed.

I said, 'No, it's not true,' and Stella turned a triumphant look on Harold, who is our resident religious maniac. Declan, the failed priest, doesn't really count because his problems were – are – purely sexual.

'This year we are going to put on our very own show. *Babes In The Wood*. I'm telling you this now before the announcement goes up on the notice-board.'

Connie gave a little scream of excitement. She used to be on the boards herself, with one of those old-fashioned touring tent shows. She loves talking about her family theatrical background. Then her lower lip began to tremble. 'Mummy always used to stand in the wings. You can do it, Connie, you can do it, she always used to say.'

Harold said, 'Play not the harlot, neither paint thy face nor deck thy limbs in the fashion of the lustful Moabites.'

Stella said, 'I've got something that'll fit you perfectly. You're a size twelve, aren't you?'

Lyle stood up and walked over to the piano. He's a tall man with flaking skin, who rarely speaks.

I said, 'Not just at the moment, Lyle, if you don't mind. We're having a discussion. Why don't you join in for a change?'

He sat down on the stool and spread his fingers on the closed lid. I pretended to ignore him, but I could feel the tiny key in my pocket burning through the fabric. It's so much easier always to give in, as with children, but then there's that dividing line, isn't there? I know some of the nurses treat the lot of them as difficult infants, most of the time, but I'm not like that and I think Dr Beck appreciates that.

I said, 'It's up to us all to make it a success. Even the staff are joining in.'

Fergus said, 'Are *you* dressing up, as well? Are you?' His eyes were shining.

'That's up to Dr Beck. He used to act at university, you know.'

Stella said, 'They'll take all the best parts, wait and see. And then get pissed afterwards at that disco out at The Pheasant, like last year. Nobody fit for work for a week. Darkie Dobbs told us about it.'

'Nurse Dobbs says more than his prayers,' I said, with more venom than I intended.

They laughed at that, except Harold and Lyle, whose head now rested sideways on the curved veneer of the piano lid. It seemed what I had said was funny, or perhaps it was the way I had said it, and I knew it was foolish of me, but I felt pleased. In that instant I saw myself as someone genuinely entertaining in their eyes and confidence took hold again. I suppose you could say I'm as much a child as any of them, and maybe that's why I go along with their games.

Looking back on it now, that was a happy time. We were innocent, harming no one, but then it all changed, as though the time had come to put away childish things. But, that particular morning, it seemed as though our little group would always be the way it was. The thought so cheered me that I went over to the old Bechstein upright and unlocked it for Lyle. The others groaned loudly but I knew that it was just a token response. Then I sat down in one of the armchairs and Connie brought me a cup of coffee from the trolley by the window.

'Thank you, Connie,' I said, and she blushed, as always. I took it from her before her hand started to shake too much. Connie has a crush on me, if that's the word, but there's nothing about it to ever get out of hand. She's still that terrified little girl peeping through the torn velvet curtains at the crowd in the tent for the evening performance of *East Lynne*. Every night of her life dying of fright while old Fay, her mother, watches from the wings. Poor Connie, when the curtain came down for the last time, it was the end of everything for her. Nobody had ever allowed her outside into the real world, you see, so how could she be expected to cope? I should mention that sometimes we do talk about such things among ourselves and Dr Beck encourages it, as long as it doesn't go too deep into old wounds. He prefers handling that side of things himself.

14

Fergus said, 'What about a game?' and, teasing, I said, 'Old Maid? Draughts? Ludo?'

He cried, 'No, no, no!' jumping to his feet. 'You know what I mean!'

Stella groaned loudly, but began to bundle her knitting away. 'Do we have to? Remember Declan can't play.'

'Well, perhaps just this once, if he promises to behave himself.' I looked across at Declan who was hunched in his chair smiling secretively to himself as usual, his hands buried to the wrists in his pockets. We stared at those twin bumps on the alert for any illicit movement, even Connie, who is prudish to an extreme.

'Declan.'

The right hand bulge palpitated slightly, then stilled under our scrutiny.

Stella said, 'You know what Dr Beck told you,' and Harold joined in with, 'And the thing that Onan did displeased the Lord and He – '

'All right, Harold, none of us is perfect.' That was me, sounding like the oldest person there and, come to think of it, it might well have been true, mentally, perhaps.

'Right. Who's going to start, then?' I cried, for everyone was suddenly on their feet moving their chairs closer. Only Lyle sat at the piano still, hands poised in the same frozen gesture above the keys.

'Lyle, come and join us.'

He called out bitterly, 'If you can't hear it, what's the point? Why bother? Why should I bother?'

I went over to him and gently closed and locked the lid. 'Lyle,' I said quietly, 'I promise I'll get a tuner tomorrow, if you come and join us.'

He looked at me. 'Tomorrow? Promise? You really promise?'

'Tomorrow.' It was a lie, of course. The piano would never be tuned, just as Lyle would never play a note on it. Like so much in

15

this place, it existed only in the imagination.

'Well?' I said. 'Have we decided?' and Connie signalled excitedly. They were seated in a semi-circle, chairs touching, and once again I was reminded of children and innocence. That's only me, I suppose, because, picture the scene in that room: the sleepers around the walls, the TV watchers and the starers into space, and then this handful of grown men and one woman pushing and shoving one another with clumsy hands.

'I've got one!' cried Connie, impatient to begin, and I knew I had to be careful she didn't get too excited. It could happen so easily for she was like a flame, strong and constant one moment, dying the next.

'Do you want to tell me?'

'Oh, yes, please!' and, running across, she put her mouth close to my ear. She smelt of old-fashioned eau de cologne and mothballs. 'The lovely lady went to the ball in a carriage and pair,' she whispered.

'That's very good, Connie, very good.'

'Really? You really think so?'

'Really,' and she left me still feeling strange from that sudden moistness in my ear.

It may well have been Connie herself who first proposed this harmless diversion to while away the time one morning or afternoon between meal-times. She was always so enthusiastic whenever it was suggested and always wanted to carry on after the others had lost interest. I looked at her now sitting erect in her chair, bright-eyed and flushed. Fergus was next to her, his hands in hers, then Stella, Harold, George, Lyle and, finally, Declan. Oh, no, I thought, and went over and made him change places, putting him next to Stella. She wouldn't stand for any of his nonsense, and was liable to cuff him heartily if he tried introducing any of his filthy little variations. That had been the cause of his being banned in the first place.

'Are we all set?'

'Yes, oh, yes!' Connie answered for everyone, and quickly pressed her mouth close to Fergus's ear. He stared straight ahead with a look of extreme concentration on his face that didn't alter, even after Connie had delivered her precious message and withdrawn to her upright position. He just sat there with his big countryman's hands spread on the knees of his trousers, brow furrowed and sweating. The others started to twist restlessly in their chairs, glaring at him, but were forbidden to speak, for that was one of the rules of the game. I gestured to Connie. She mouthed a second time. Fergus began to nod faster and faster as though something miraculous had been entrusted to him. Finally, with a sigh, he leaned close to Declan and, for a quick moment, Declan looked across at me. He grinned but I kept my face stern. Then, putting his hand over his mouth in what I can only describe as a gesture worthy of Frank Dobbs, he transferred Connie's sentence to Stella. She listened, then looked hard at him as though he might well be up to his old tricks. But, no, it seemed he was blameless, for, finally, Stella bent her head to whisper to Harold, and so it travelled to George and then to Lyle at the end of the row. This was the moment everyone had been waiting for, particularly Connie, who could barely sit still with excitement.

Lyle stood up but, instead of announcing the message as he was supposed to, he looked around him with an expression of contempt on his face. 'Don't you know I have a concert in two weeks' time? Why should I play these stupid games when I could be practising? Answer me that. Don't you know I need at least five hours a day if I'm to be ready?'

Connie burst into tears and Fergus soon joined her. Stella got to her feet with clenched fists: the right had a dagger and crown tattooed on it. Declan sniggered.

I shouted, 'Lyle! Lyle Donaghy, you will be *good*!' and at that moment Dr Beck's soft voice sounded behind me. 'Dear, oh, dearie me, what have we here?'

He had come in quietly, as always, and from his tone must have been watching and listening for some little time. I had got so excited myself I hadn't noticed how silent the rest of the room had become. He has that effect, has Dr Beck, even on the most hopeless of his cases.

'It's only a game,' I said, and the moment I spoke I realised I had betrayed something important.

He stood there, immaculate as always, with only his row of pens breaking the perfect whiteness of his doctor's coat. A different colour for each of his personal codes that none of us has ever been able to decipher, try as we will.

'What do you call this game? Does it have a name?'

I couldn't answer, because as far as I was concerned it was something exclusive to the group.

'It must have a name. Surely, now?' Dr Beck was smiling in that way he has, infinitely patient, and quite prepared to wait for an answer for as long as it might take. I looked at Connie, but her tears were still flowing. Then a voice from the back of the room said, 'Chinese Whispers'.

A stranger stood there. He must have come in with the Doctor, a pale young man with dark hair, wearing a tweed jacket and brown cord trousers. I couldn't tell whether he was a doctor or a patient; he seemed more like a doctor, but then Beck said, 'Well done, Gavin,' and I knew I was wrong. 'Come and meet everybody.' The stranger walked over and stood beside him.

'This is Gavin who's going to join you. I know you'll all want to make him feel at home. I think he's been looking forward to meeting you.' He turned to the young man. 'Isn't that so, Gavin?'

I saw that there was something odd about the stranger's hair, the way it was cut, as though someone had taken something sharp to it in a fit of rage or something equally violent. It had been carefully brushed to cover up the worst ravages but on one side his razor had started an inch and a half on the high side. He didn't seem in the least put out by it and stood there with a smile on his face. It wasn't really a smile you could warm to; it had that same lack of depth as Dr Beck's. And, as the two of them continued to stand there, they did begin to look as though they were on an equal footing, after all. On the other hand, I felt as if I was being lumped in with the others, still in their chairs, waiting to be dismissed. It was disloyal of me, I knew, but there was nothing I could do about it. Then Stella, never one to be inhibited, blurted out, 'When are we going to be told about the panto? He' – pointing at me – 'won't go into details. We should be consulted, you know.'

Dr Beck continued smiling. 'But, of course, and you will, never fear, just as soon as those details have been finalised. Kenny here knows as little about it as you do. That's why he's being so mysterious. Isn't that so, Kenny?'

Everybody was suddenly looking at me as though in a new light, and it was a moment in my life, believe me, when it seemed as though things would never be the same again. There was nothing for me to say, of course, and the moment passed. Dr Beck went off on a little tour of the other patients in the room, but I knew it was only for appearances' sake, nothing more than some smiles and nods and worthless little pats, and then out of the door as soon as was decently possible. As he was leaving, I saw him look over across the heads at the new young man who was standing with his hands in his pockets as though he had already mastered the geography of the place. They exchanged smiles and the door closed behind the Doctor.

Then, almost as though he had been waiting for this moment to bring his own mocking finale to the game, Lyle cried out in a harsh voice, 'Mrs O'Grady suffered a fall from her brand new wheelchair!' and the whole room fell silent at the violence in his tones.

Connie screamed and rushed at him. He was still standing by the locked piano and he suffered her puny fists on his chest with no change in his look of contempt until I took hold of her. She collapsed the instant my hands touched her. By this time the panic had spread, as often happens. Sobbing had broken out in several quarters of the room and one of the sleepers in the outer ring was banging his head rhythmically on a window-ledge. A coffee-table went over and with it the draughts board and all its pieces. The two players, both sweet-looking old men, lunged forward at each other's throats. I knew I had trouble on my hands and rang the bell for help. I remember thinking at the time how do I know if this is really working or not. It gave off no sound for one to tell and this was the first time I had ever been forced to make use of it.

Then Dobbs and one of the other nurses arrived, running, and began to push people back into their chairs – without much delicacy, I may add, but in the circumstances I was in no mood to protest. My own little group sat with their chairs together at the still heart of all this commotion. Stella stared straight ahead at some distant point beyond the picture windows. She had retrieved her needles and wool and seemed to be waiting for the moment to resume. Declan was slouched, both hands busy at their favourite pastime; Fergus wept; Harold glowered and George had that look on his face, as always, that went with those far-off dialling tones sounding in his head. Connie and Lyle stood a little apart near the piano. She had her thumb in her mouth for comfort and he seemed oblivious to everything he had sparked off.

Finally order was restored and Dobbs changed channels on the television until he found a programme on underwater exploration. In a little while the room began to fall under the spell of all those gently moving fish, and the hiss of escaping air bubbles was the only sound to be heard.

20

As for myself, no moving pictures on a screen, no matter how pretty they happened to be, were about to shift the mood I was in. I looked around the room for someone or something to blame it on, and my eyes settled on the group still in their same positions. They seemed to have forgotten everything that had just taken place, the way children do, and then I looked over to the window where the stranger was standing. There was nothing childish about the grin on his face. It was directed at me, I could see that, and there and then I should have known that a new and cruel element had entered our little world.

The funny thing was that when I first heard about him – even coming, as it did, from the lips of Frank Dobbs – I had looked forward to this moment. I knew all about our celebrity – well, as much as anyone on the staff – his case, even though it had been in the papers five years previously, still stayed with people. In a small place like ours it's hard to forget something like that. In a way, the fact that the killing had nothing to do with politics or religion, like the others we keep hearing about these days, somehow made it more shocking in retrospect.

It all came back to me as I faced the murderer now across the room, for, he had confessed, hadn't he? The papers told how he had broken down and begged forgiveness for something he couldn't remember doing at the time. Scotland Yard's most famous man had been brought over specially to get him to that point – it took days, not weeks – and then another London expert told the court the young man in the dock was insane and not responsible for his actions. That's how he came to be here, now, in Willis Wing upstairs, ever since that day.

I may as well admit that the case had a strange and fascinating effect on me at the time. I kept thinking, morbidly, perhaps, that it could have been me there in the dock. We were the same age, both of us lonely and mixed up about life and sex – all of *that* discussed publicly and at great length. I began to hate those

21

lawyers and reporters and London experts flown in for the day, giving their views on someone they had never known and would never care to think about again. Once I even went as far as to cycle to the courthouse; it wasn't such a great distance from where I lived at the time. A vague and foolish idea had got into my head that I might be able to give support in some way, but my

courage deserted me when I saw all those women in headscarves outside crying for blood.

You may think it strange that I should identify with someone who had stabbed a young girl to death – twenty times, so the papers said – in a damp, dark wood. The truth of the matter was, I didn't believe he had done it. Like a great machine that can't be

23

stopped once set in motion, evidence like that was bound to crush anyone, even someone as innocent as me, for that matter. I was able to put myself in a stranger's place, someone I had never set eyes on. There was a photograph, of course; it looked like a holiday snap the papers had somehow got hold of. There he was beside a Scottish loch in happier circumstances smiling for the family album. I recognised the same nervous grin I must have worn myself at that age. It only served to strengthen my belief.

And the foolish thing was that, right at this moment, over five years later, I wanted to go across to this stranger and tell him that I still believed in him, no matter what people said or what he himself had been forced into confessing.

But the look on his face stopped me, and I began to move about the room just as Dr Beck had done earlier, but without the smiles or the little pats. I felt nervous and slightly lost. My real place was at the heart of the room, but there was nothing to take me there, I could see that. My little group was lost to me, their dulled eyes fixed on the wonders of the Great Barrier Reef.

I left them with a television voice intoning, '. . . a million years of darkness in these eerie, underwater depths'. I hadn't the heart to look over at the newcomer, but I knew he was still standing by the window, as though he had been there all his life.

THREE

Cycling home that evening, my usual route up the old back drive, I was soon soaked under those overhanging and dripping boughs. Each cold drop seemed to have been suspended in wait there all day. It was dark, as well, but I was used to that, no light for miles, just trees hemming me in. I used to wonder had they been planted in such abundance like that to keep the patients *in*, or was it to keep outsiders *out*? It's a bit like living in a foreign country, middle-European, perhaps. The association that comes to mind is one of those fairy-tale settings, of the sort I used to read about when I was younger, the sound of wolves always a distinct possibility. But perhaps that's a shade on the fanciful side. Once beyond the walls, built in Famine times, the countryside around here is very different in appearance, flat and rolling, for the most part.

I pushed on, the wheels making heavy work of the wet gravel. There are frequent potholes – most of them I've memorised – but tonight my recall seemed faulty for some reason. Still, I had less than a mile to travel, for I have to tell you that, strictly speaking, I live within the grounds. A year ago Dr Beck was kind enough to get the management committee to agree to my mobile home going on to a piece of cleared ground near the back gates. It's an *Ambassador S*, aluminium body, thirty-two footer, with bathroom and shower, although that's not a lot of use with no water at hand. There's no electricity either, but I manage. When mother died I bought it with the little money she left – there were just the two of us – because I'd always had this romantic notion of a caravan and the rolling road. Well, that part of it wasn't sensible; I'm certainly no gypsy, but I got the other half of the dream, and now I tell myself I couldn't bear to live under the roof of any house. It's very cosy inside with the lamp lit; there's even a real fireplace. Normally I don't use this, but tonight I felt I needed something to cheer me up, so I put a match to it. I took off my wet clothes and ate a little something and the fire was the perfect barrier between me and everything cold and miserable out there beyond the drawn curtains.

Sometimes I think it's a strange life I lead, by myself like this, and at my age, too. I've no friends, really, of any sort. It doesn't bother me, not in any distressing way. Most of the time the thought of it never even enters my head but just now and again, on nights such as these, there enters that tiny niggling doubt but, then, to coin an old-fashioned phrase, I count my blessings. Mother taught me that. Her photograph has pride of place in a silver frame on the mantelpiece. Yes, there's even one of those, too. I sat there in my armchair, in my slippers, all the comforts of home, as they say, and felt the cares of the day dissolve.

My little treasures were there in that small space and I could see them in the soft light, the family photographs and holiday souvenirs, my shelves of paperbacks and *Picturegoers*, the old oak bureau, on top of which sits my collection of miniatures. I've got over two hundred now, from every corner of the globe. People who know me always bring me new ones back from their travels. I don't have to ask any more, the doctors and most of the nurses know about the little bottles. They make jokes but, of course, I've never opened one of them and don't intend to, that would spoil the whole idea. I just love looking at them and their colours, the

28 reds and greens and yellows and the one or two beautiful blues.

There is a separate bedroom, just like in a proper house, but I prefer to sleep here on a Put-U-Up so that I can have a last look at everything before I blow out the lamp. Sometimes I listen to the radio but tonight I felt too tired even for that. I was wise enough not to mull over the events of the day and at ten or so I reckon I must have been fast asleep.

Around four in the morning I suddenly awoke and lay still with my heart pounding, not knowing why it was so. Something had disturbed me, that was obvious, but I had no idea what. The wind in the trees had dropped, as it has a habit of doing just before first light, and I listened, straining head and neck above the bed-clothes. Then something heavy landed on the roof and im-mediately rolled rapidly down its slope. It must have been a branch, I thought, broken off by the wind, but then the way it had fallen away so smoothly and weightily was not what a branch would have done. I wasn't frightened, not then, because you get used to such noises; woods are like that. Trees have their own constant conversation and there are living things as well. Cats have fought above my head and birds tap and scratch, even attempt to build nests. But in the dead of winter such things are rare.

I lay awake until morning, but even then I held back from going outside. The rain had departed and, for the first time in weeks, a bit of sun showed itself. I opened the windows, washed, dressed, had my bowl of cereal and stepped outside. There was nothing lying about that I could see, even underneath, for I got down on hands and knees to look; nothing new, that is, among all the rubbish that somehow finds its way under there. Then I brought out the bike and wheeled it across the bumpy expanse in front of the mobile home. I know people call them caravans and 'mobile home' does sound as if you're putting on airs, but I prefer to stick with that, even in my own head. Usually I stop just before I ride off for a last backward look to remind myself that I'm lucky   29 to have such a romantic setting, even in winter under bare trees, but today I didn't feel like it. Something was nagging at me; I thought at first it was that bump in the night but then, about a hundred yards along the drive, I realised that today, Thursday, was my day off. Right there in the middle of the track I put on the brakes and for a minute I stared down into a puddle. I had that lost feeling again, the one I'd had yesterday in the recreation room.

I didn't want to go back home – there was something of a defeat about that – so I rode on but, instead of taking my usual route, I kept going until I reached the main road that leads to town. It's somewhere I try to avoid if I can because it's no longer that magic place I used to visit with mother.

Each Saturday we would travel in on the bus with the other country people and the day would be spent in leisurely fashion going around the shops. Sometimes I would get a haircut. I always associate that with those weekly trips, somehow. There were only two barbers in town, I remember, but mother always preferred the one in the Market Square, even though his hands shook and his breath smelt of surgical spirit. Then to round off the day we would go to the solitary cinema and with stinging scalp I would sit in the darkness and keep company with Doris and Donald, Mario, Kathryn, Mitzi and Judy.

Those old technicoloured musicals we enjoyed so much in the cinema together must have combined to create a world which could never be the same again. But, despite that, I steered the bicycle on past the first bungalows, strung out at first, then coming closer together as the Catholic church hove in sight, then the fire station, the public weighbridge, the start of the town proper. The narrow streets were choked with traffic. It was market day, I realised; lorries, loose boxes and tractors much in evidence. There seemed to be a lot of noise, more than I could bear. I began to feel nervous but didn't want to dismount for I felt that would make me look conspicuous, wheeling my machine on the pavement.

I remembered the last time I had been here, a summer afternoon, early-closing. It had been Dr Beck's idea and I had tried to tell him I wasn't happy about bringing the group into town on an outing, but he only smiled and said, 'I have every confidence in you, Kenny. There's no one else I would dream of asking. That's between you and me.'

We drove in a hired minibus and the driver was told to be back at his vehicle by four o'clock. He was a local man named McClurg and, of course, he hadn't turned up even when the town hall clock struck the half hour. By that time Connie was in a state. She needed to get to a toilet badly, but refused to use the public ones in the square. And, looking at her twisting nervously there beside the locked van, I could see how someone with Connie's sensibilities would rather die first. She was wearing, if I recall, something totally inappropriate in heavy velvet on that hot August day. Her mother's old costumes had travelled with her and it was impossible to tell what she would be wearing next. In desperation, all I could think of was the hotel, so I hurried the group back along River Street and told them not to budge on any account until I came out again with Connie.

I led her past the two girls at the reception desk and the young, uncaring manager with his buttonhole, and they looked at us in that same hard way that everyone in this town seems to use on strangers, especially ones like us. I'd seen enough of it that day to recognise it as we trailed past those closed shops and noisy pubs. Connie seemed to spend ages and, as I waited for her on a hard chair in the hall, I kept thinking why should it have to be me, always me, with my heart in my mouth. The hotel was busy. It was always very popular with the commercial trade and laughing men in suits kept coming and going past where I sat. I tried to look as though I was also there with a purpose but I had   *31* no real idea of how to achieve such a look.

Then she appeared, smelling sweetly, and with a young girl's shy smile on her face, and we went back out on to the street. I looked around but there was no sign of the others. A couple of ruffians in anoraks were watching from a doorway, grinning, and one of them whistled as I began dragging Connie after me. I felt panicky, the river my first thought because water would surely exert a terrible pull on them, just like children, but at the bridge I could see no one. People passing in cars must have wondered at the sight of an agitated man with a woman in tow, hanging over the parapet.

Eventually, of course, I found them in the car-park, sitting inside the minibus, and they waved happily as we came into view. The driver, McClurg, was at the wheel, his head buried in the racing pages, but I was still too shocked to say anything to him. Later I found out that he had brought the group along with him as he passed the hotel on his way back from the bookie's. On the way home I stared at his freckled neck, wanting to stick a knife into its fat red folds.

The memory of that was a depressing one and soon I had had enough of the place. There was nothing for me here. I had no place or part in this bustle and activity. I wondered if some of these people milling around me might remember when it was so very different. It was all Cash 'n' Carrys, Chinese takeaways and pubs with names like The Klondike and Twin Forks. Even the cinema was no longer showing films but, instead, had bingo nightly.

Turning the bike around, I rode home feeling empty and old, like those pensioners I'd seen earlier sitting in the Burger Bar among noisy teenagers.

Next day when I got up I had an ache in my bones and a high temperature. It was the soaking the night before last, of course, followed by that profitless trip to town. Somehow I struggled into

work but Dr Beck noticed my condition at coffee break and, laying his palm on my brow in his usual absent-minded way, just as if I were another patient, suggested I go home. I wondered if he would notice if I ever came back, if it would register with anyone in the place, for that matter. That was the mood I was in. Sometimes it can have its pleasant side; any child knows that, sitting up in his room imagining the moment when everyone will be repentant, but I couldn't summon up much of that.

I got back to my place, put away the bicycle and, sweating more than usual, was about to step up and through the door when I saw something glistening in the grass. I picked up an unopened can of Harp lager and, dazed, carried it inside with me. The tablets Dr Beck had given me locked me in a stupor for the next twenty-four hours but every so often, coming out of it, I could see from my bed that ordinary enough object sitting on the bureau among the miniatures yet, because of the circumstances, it might well have come from outer space. Indeed, I had a series of dreams where I seemed to be following its trajectory through miles and miles of empty atmosphere. It sped before me as if with a mind of its own and something told me I must not lose sight or track of it. My life depended on it. On and on the silvery bullet flew and the further it travelled the greater my desperation grew . . .

It was only when the effects of the tablets had worn off and I was on my feet again that the mystery of how that beer can had come to land on my roof began to really worry me.

FOUR

On Monday morning I was back on duty and as I walked along the corridors with their familiar scents and sounds it was like returning to school again after the holidays, that mixture of relief and dread in equal parts. At some point I saw Dobbs before he could see me and I drew back until he passed on out of sight. He was whistling merrily without a care in the world. I thought of the weight of evil he should have been carrying but wasn't. There are so many things I try to understand but never can.

One of the patients, a woman, well-known to all of us, stopped me on the third floor. Usually I'm prepared and, murmuring, 'Yes, Mary, I know, Mary, I know,' I would simply brush past her. Today, for some reason, I allowed her hand to reach out and touch, then hold me. I turned my head away – her scent is gamey, to say the least – and she whispered loudly, 'Doctor, you must help me. It's getting worse, oh, much worse. I didn't get any sleep, they had me up all night. What can I do with six of them? Tell me that. In here.' She patted her old woman's belly. 'It's meat they want. That's what they say; meat, meat, not enough meat. Oh, doctor, doctor.'

Pulling free, I left her there, her voice starting to climb. '*Meat, meat, meat!*' The cry seemed to carry down the staircases, following me until I stood outside the door that leads to the men's lavatories in the basement. There I bent and unlaced my shoes as   *37*

I had done countless times before, pushed open the door and tiptoed in as quietly as any husband returning home from a night on the tiles. Then I saw that the doors facing me were open. I looked at my watch but there was no mistake. A tap dripped and a cistern hissed and I stood there alone in the middle of that cold, ugly, echoing place with my shoes in my hand. For the first and last time it came to me what a ridiculous sight I must look if someone were to come in. It didn't strike me that perhaps Fergus was sick or had been delayed in some way. I just felt I had been made a fool of.

I left the place determined to do something about it. For one thing, I wouldn't be quite so understanding or eager next time. No, Dr Beck, I'm sorry, I heard myself say, it's quite out of the question. Some of us have been putting a lot more into the job than we're given credit for. It seems to me there's a definite lack of appreciation in that department. My duties are set out quite specifically and no one knows them better than you. From now on let's just keep them like that, shall we? I went upstairs rehearsing my new outlook on life.

On the second floor there came the sound of a piano being played, something light and rhythmic, a tango, it sounded like, and I stopped to listen. At first it seemed as if it might be a recording of some kind but then the player stumbled over a phrase and repeated it. Still it didn't dawn on me, it was much too fantastic and, as well, the new mood I was in wouldn't allow me to believe such a thing. But then I opened the door of the recreation room and there was no longer any doubt. The music was coming from the old piano. Lyle was sitting at its keyboard frowning but, nevertheless, pounding confidently away. A space had been cleared among the chairs and couples were dancing. I recognised Stella and one of the livelier of the male patients, a small man with a moustache and a shiny bald head. They looked surprisingly expert, and Stella had on a glittering tight outfit in maroon I'd never seen before. Then I saw Connie and Fergus, and Declan and a young girl with short dyed hair from another floor. He was holding her much too tightly, of course, and there was that disgusting leer on his face, but she looked as though she didn't mind.

I stood there looking around for some clue as to how and why this was happening, and then I saw the cause. It – or rather, *he* – was standing at the window just as I had last seen him, with that self-same grin spread across his face. He was the one I should have headed for but, instead, I moved through the chairs to the centre of the room out of habit. Connie saw me and, breaking away from her partner, ran across. 'You must dance with me, say you will! You will, won't you? Oh, say you will!' and she put her hot hands in mine. There was sweat on her upper lip and Stella's mascara – it certainly wasn't her own – had started to run in a trickle from the corner of one eye. She was wearing another of her mother's dated creations, this time in satin, with a froth of lace about the bust and upper arms. This was no spur of the moment whim, I realised. Someone had spent a deal of time on her hair as well. I felt sickened by the deceit of it all. Pulling my hand away, I suddenly felt hard and unforgiving towards her. She looked pathetic for someone her age and her English accent, so prim and proper, grated on me.

'Tell me, how did Lyle get the piano open?'

She giggled. 'Oh, but it wasn't Lyle. You'll never guess what he did. He, Gavin, took a little – '

I crossed to the piano then and stood looking down at the keyboard. Lyle's fingers were long and delicate, something I'd never noticed before. He was concentrating with moist lips and a frown just like a child. I took the tiny key out of my pocket and laid it carefully down on top of the lid. The moment its metal touched the shiny wood his touch began to falter, until finally he stopped playing altogether. A silence so painful followed from every part

39

of the room – only then did I notice that the television's sound had been turned right down, something unheard of – that I felt at any minute Dobbs and the other nurses must come bursting in, for it was as if an alarm had been set off, a silent one, but of the most urgent and penetrating kind.

Then Stella, tall, broad-shouldered Stella, her warpaint barely masking the blue shaving shadow, began to clap, a slow, insulting beat that was soon taken up around the room. My face blazed, I could feel it, and my eyes darted here and there seeking out enemies. But they were all against me, it seemed, even some of those on the outer rim I had always taken for hopeless cases. It could have been that it was only the noise that had touched something deep in them, it could have been that, like sleepers restlessly stirring. I told myself that later but, at the time, no such consolation was forthcoming. At the door I looked back; a mistake, but how could I help myself? Connie was weeping and Lyle was staring down at his hands. Everyone else continued to clap except for that lone figure by the window, the outsider with the grin. I closed the door and leaned my back against it. The wood trembled slightly and, feeling its throb, I told myself I had got it wrong: *I* was the outsider now.

It wasn't the end of the world, of course; nothing ever is. I still had a job and I did it as I had been trained to do, but there were no longer any of those little games to lighten the day, even the ones I used to groan about.

The days seemed longer as well and I found it more of a strain keeping out of Dobbs' and his cronies' way. They rarely if ever came near the recreation room but now I was forced to roam the corridors as they did. I found myself spending more and more time behind barred doors in the basement lavatory. Now it was my turn to sit there facing the painted wood just as Fergus had once done. Head in hand, I would will myself into a state of near stupefaction so that the time might pass more quickly. It was difficult to avoid what was written on the walls and scratched into the wood in front of me. One day I saw my own name there amongst all that filth. What certain people thought of me, one in particular, I guessed, was something I had grown to accept but, seeing it printed there, for all to read, gave me a shiver of horror. I scraped it away, of course, but the damage had been done. I knew I wouldn't be able to rest now until I had paid a visit to every single cubicle to satisfy myself. At last I had found something to take my mind off the moment when I would have to go upstairs again, for certain duties still had to be fulfilled.

At medication time I would position the drugs trolley near the door; the window used to be the place for that, but *he* was always there now, and they would shuffle past holding out their paper cups. It used to be a time for jokes, much rattling of the pills like dice. I recalled how that never seemed to lose its appeal. Now it was like doling out sweets to a line of mutes. None of them would speak or look at me, or at what I shook into their cups, for that matter. With one exception. *He* would stroll across in leisurely fashion to join the tail of the queue, I would drop his Lithium into his cup for him to swallow but, unlike the others, first he would stare down at the little coloured capsules, then pointedly at the drugs register open on the flap of the trolley, then at me. It was his way of reminding me of his superiority, that he wasn't like the rest of them who would gulp down anything I cared to dish out, and he would stand there until I had ticked off his name in the ledger. Only then would he toss off his dose and walk away. For the first time I began to worry about something I had been doing unthinkingly until then. Checking and double-checking dosage against each patient's name became a new obsession. I would start feeling nervous the moment he joined the line and my hand would start to shake. Once he hesitated – deliberately, of course – as I reached out to transfer the contents of my cup to his, and the sound of my shame seemed to fill the room. Putting the cup to his

MAURICE LEITCH

lips, he swallowed and grinned at me. I shouted, 'Open your
mouth! Open your mouth, I say!' and the room went quiet. It was
so unfair, for everyone knew I had to make certain they
swallowed their medicine and didn't carry it around in their
mouths, as some tried to do.

And so it went on like that until I began to dread even opening
the door of the recreation room in the morning. Reaching out for
the handle, I would try to control my panic. Then, having grasped
the cold metal, I would listen, hoping for some advantage, some
indication of their mood, like a child outside a classroom. On
occasions I could hear laughter, Stella's deep voice figuring
strongly, but I could sometimes make out Connie's giggle too and,
once, was certain I could distinguish all of them in chorus, hard
as that may seem. That was the bitterest blow. A moment later
would come the low rise and fall of that softest, most persuasive of
tones. He rarely spoke in my presence, but I know it was his voice.
However, I could never make out what was being said, so God
knows what disgusting stuff he was feeding those innocents.

One particular day I opened the door and there they were at the
window, sitting at his feet, as it were, and, of course, everything
stopped, as it always did, as if at some pre-arranged signal. George
no longer dialled his imaginary numbers in the air; someone, it
wasn't hard to guess who, had provided him with an ancient
black handset, and Lyle would often strike a few defiant chords on
the ever-open piano. Today he didn't even bother to acknowledge
my presence. So, it had come to this, I thought, giving my
imitation of an invisible man, picking my way among the
outstretched legs of the sleepers. I straightened a picture on the
wall, pretending interest in the Donegal landscape, three-
quarters sky, the rest muddy browns and greens, but secretly I
was looking towards the window.

I had to admit the change in the man was certainly a dramatic
one, his appearance, not the personality – that was something he

carried with him untouched wherever he went: I didn't need to be told that. He was wearing a navy blue guernsey, white shirt, twill trousers, and his hair was presentable again. Out of spite I remembered what it had been like the first time he had stood there alongside Dr Beck. Now he had the look of someone sure of himself and of his place in the world, even in this off-centre world, someone who could only be called Gavin. The parents who had chosen the name would be content if they could see a photograph of him as he was just now, so straight, so confident. I remembered that healthy pink tongue he had stuck out for my inspection.

Oh, why did it have to be like this? I asked myself. No animosity ever existed on my part. Far from it. I was, wasn't I, the one who had believed in him when everyone else was calling him some kind of monster? If we'd only met then, and it wasn't so unthinkable either, living, as we did, not so far apart, two lonely boys growing up in a hard, unsympathetic world. But then I thought of that house of his parents by the sea . . . I had never seen it, but I could tell what it was like – the grounds, the gate-lodge, perhaps a rolled tennis court. His father, after all, was a retired English major and people like that always found the best places, places out of bounds to someone like me, the son of a mill-worker.

I looked at my reflection in the darker part of the picture, low among the piles of turf and still bog water. There were shadows under my eyes. My skin looked blotchy, too. The gulf between the man holding court by the window and the one staring back at me seemed never so wide.

There was a reason, however, for the way I looked. For the past week I had been waking up suddenly in the middle of the night sweating and anxiously waiting for something to happen. A bump overhead, I suppose, but although I lay there until early light, no more beer cans were to fall from the heavens. Once, I felt certain, I did hear movement out there among the dark trees, and another night, a laugh, it sounded like, distant and unpleasant. The pattern was a worrying one. I started to take something to send me deeper into sleep.

Then one night, a Sunday it was, and some days after the time I've been describing, my doubts were dispelled. At about three in the morning my alarm clock fell and stopped. A nightmare from some film or other in which I was falling, trapped inside a locked car, seemed to have come true, for I found myself on the floor. The walls were shaking. I heard my miniatures dropping from their shelves; pictures followed, then the unwashed crockery from the table. Still drowsy from the effects of the pill I had taken, I tried to stand up but everything was tilting as in a storm at sea. Yet there was no wind outside; it was a calm, clear night in the grip of frost.

But then I heard the sounds of effort and it came home to me that someone, more than one, certainly, was rocking the trailer. I screamed, I couldn't help myself, and all movement ceased. Holding on to the side of the bed settee, I felt as if my time had come, for the sound of my voice, high and pitiful, hadn't the power to chase anyone away. Surely it must have the opposite effect. That was what I believed and, convinced of it, I told myself that I would put up no resistance for that would only inflame the brutes further. I had a mental picture of their palms flat against the frosty metal, preparing themselves for that ferocious final push, three or four unshaven locals: I probably knew them by sight. At any rate, they most certainly knew me, for hadn't they been sniffing around for the best part of a week, eyes and ears trained for my slightest movement? I thought of them listening out there and of what must have come their way on those bitter November nights, the radio playing quietly or, as a bonus, my own voice, for I do admit I talk to myself, just like anyone else used to living on their own.

My senses seemed never so sharp as I crouched there in
44 pyjamas on the floor; hearing, much more, for obvious reasons,

but I could also smell the carpet and its dust in painful close-up: something else, as well, the sweet scent of aniseed. It grew and grew until it masked all else and then a further small explosion broke the silence, and I knew what it was. Another of my beloved miniatures had fallen from its place on the shelf and shattered, and presently the essence of coffee came to my nostrils.

I am a coward, that must be plain by this time, but still I got to my feet, went to the door and pulled back the bolt. The cold cut like a knife, yet I stood there exposed in the doorway, daring them, whoever they were, to get on with what they had in mind. They could do what they wished with me; I was at their mercy. A strange calmness had taken over. I felt purged of fear. The moon was high and I remained there in its light, with a certain nobility, I thought. The whole clearing was bright as day, but the only shadows were those of trees. Perhaps my yell had chased them off. People of their type, I consoled myself, were invariably supposed to be cowards, sneaks in the night – they were, weren't they? I could bear the chill no longer and closed the door.

Careful of my bare feet for the first time, I felt my way across to the lamp and put a match to the wick and it was as if I'd come home to a burglary. But the humiliation seemed much worse, somehow, to have been molested from the *outside*, the way someone might contemptuously shake a doll's house. Pictures, books, magazines, all my miniatures, lay strewn across the carpet. In the kitchenette beyond lay a worse mess. Every cupboard door swung open and a white drift of something granular spread its way underfoot from wall to wall. Crockery and utensils had been shaken loose from their hooks. But why make an inventory? I looked around at the destruction and had no heart to touch a thing.

I must have sat there on the edge of the bed for an hour, maybe more, then I got up, pulled some clothes over my pyjamas and went outside. Half-heartedly I played at detective but there were no footprints or other signs I could make out on the hard ground. It felt like iron through the thin soles of my slippers and I hobbled across to a softer place under a tree. Leaning with my back against its bark, I felt like a stranger and, my home, from where I stood, seemed even more foreign. For the first time I saw how out of place it really was, deposited like that in the middle of the raw countryside; that it must look like that to other people as well. Was it possible the attack had been directed at *it* and not the person inside, out of some obscure resentment to do with its structure and position? I told myself I was being fanciful. Whoever they were, they hadn't come all this way just for a bout of vandalism. They could have found something in that line much closer to home. No, it was me they were after.

I must explain something of the history of the place – the hospital, I mean – and of the town, too, for that matter, for that has a bearing on these things as well. It was, to begin with, a mansion of sorts, but its outer walls only came later, in famine times, built as a form of outdoor relief by and for the starving poor of the town. They laboured at something they must have resented bitterly, block upon block translated into bread. Those same walls put up to last were to stand as a reminder, a cruel one, if you like, of bad times. Later still, the original family sold up house and estate and it became the local Poorhouse, and yet again that ring of stone, Antrim basalt, black as pitch when wet, only served to remind the town further of its shame. It's still called the 'Poorhouse Wall' to this day, by the way. Finally, it was taken over as an insane asylum, which is how it ended up as it is today. So, while those dark old walls still stand, the townspeople will always have something to feel bitter about. That resentment has existed for as long as I can remember, even on the part of those who travel each day to work in its kitchens or its grounds. I suppose if they had their way they'd never set foot inside the place but, when the big man-made fibres company closed its factory gates five years ago, what else were they to do?

This may help to explain why they hate us so much, doctors, patients, nurses – yes, even someone like myself who was brought up amongst them. I thought of those hard faces I'd seen that day I walked my crocodile of harmless cases along the main street on Dr Beck's orders. I'd tried to tell him of those long memories but, of course, he wouldn't, couldn't, concern himself with such things. I could well imagine what he would have to say if I tried telling him about this business.

'My dear Kenny, in the wee small hours each and every one of us is at his most vulnerable, prey to the most alarming fantasies. You've been on night-duty: what you've seen and heard must surely convince you of that phenomenon. Why should you, then, be any exception?'

But it wasn't in my imagination, any of it, and a moment later what I nearly stepped in was certainly no fantasy. There it lay in the open, shameful and still warm, I felt sure of that, without having to put it to the test. I went back to the trailer, found a spade and buried it right where one of my night visitors had dropped it, his crude calling-card. The ground was frozen and I was sweating by the time the job was done. Before going in I took the soiled spade and hurled it as far away from me as I could into the trees.

Then I went inside and opened one of the miniatures that lay on the floor. It was a new experience, I have to confess; not only had I never been tempted before, but I must admit also I'd never tasted anything stronger than pale sherry. Mother had never allowed the stuff into the house. Only after I'd drunk it and felt its warm, spreading glow did I look at the label. It was a sweet liqueur from Corfu, and its attractive yellow colour was what must have drawn me in the first place to where it lay among all the other tiny bottles scattered over the carpet.

I lay on the bed feeling relaxed and sleepy, eyeing them lying there like so many fallen jewels in the lamplight. Why shouldn't I enjoy them? I told myself, and I took up another. This was a mistake despite its beautiful ruddy tint, for it turned out to be an unpleasant tasting Italian bitters. I rinsed away its traces with a green Chartreuse and after that remembered nothing more until next day.

The lamp had burned itself out when I awoke, but the room was bright with sunlight streaming through a gap in the curtains to remind me that I hadn't had a nightmare, despite what the good Doctor might have to say. It was all too real, the disorder; even proof of the exact time it had taken place, if I'd needed it, was there in the shape of the broken alarm-clock. The hands had stopped at four minutes past three. It was a Mickey Mouse alarm I'd had beside my bed since my first day at grammar school. Mother had bought it in Woolworth's and now its useful life was at an end. Such were the thoughts that passed through my brain in an orderly stream; the headache was to come later. Then the flow hit something jagged and terrifying – *my God*, I thought, *what's the real time?* Not even stopping to wash or shave – I would have to do both later – I dragged on my clothes, rushed outside and set off. The door, I knew, had been left unlocked, but the thought didn't concern me as much as it might have done. What did was that for the first time in the five years I'd been in my job I was going to be late for duty, three hours at that.

Pedalling up the back drive, I had the risen sun square in my eyes and it was also as though a new pattern of potholes had formed during the night. My front wheel kept aiming for them and finding them.

I got to the hospital and my luck seemed to hold; I even had time to get into a white coat without anyone seeing me. But then, on the way down to the basement lavatories with my toothbrush and my razor in my pocket, I heard a voice calling out, 'Kenny, *there* you are!' There was no need to turn, the tones were unmistakable. I should also mention that no one else calls me by that boyish name, not even mother when she was alive.

'Kenny, what an elusive creature you are, to be sure, and just when I wanted to congratulate you, too.'

I did turn then and the shock on my face must have been obvious for he laughed. 'Yes, congratulations. That's what I said.'

He was close enough by now to take me by the sleeve and once again I could smell his doctor's smell, that expensive cologne so many of them seem to use, nothing remotely like antiseptic, but something exclusive, setting them apart. His skin was always closely shaven as well, tanned and taut and unblemished.

'I don't really care how you did it, the results are what matters. Such a change, such a regeneration! What a dark old horse you are. Not a word all this time.'

We walked along the cold corridor – all that high gloss paint in apple-green – and the pain in my head seemed to be getting much worse.

'I don't mind telling you I was beginning to feel sceptical. I mean, all that indulgence, those childish games, such primitive therapy, really, if you can even call it that.'

I had this strange feeling that I didn't exist any more, that people had started to talk around, over, through me. It had been going on for some little time, too, a sort of spreading infection that sooner or later affected everyone I came into contact with. I tried to think of when and how it could have started, the first symptom of my eventual disappearance. Of course it was mainly the hangover talking, I was to realise that afterwards but, at the time, being guided along that corridor like that, I felt as insubstantial and light as air.

But then Beck said, 'And, of course, no one sings your praises more than Gavin,' and it was as if I'd missed something important. I stopped, I couldn't help myself. He looked at me.

'He tells me the two of you are quite a little team already. Every day something new, isn't that the way of it?'

His voice slowed. He was looking at me as if I had materialised for the first time. In his eyes, dark and shining like the rest of him, I could see what must be registering, the stubble, the disordered hair, my own eyes, certainly bloodshot. He said, 'Well, once again, congratulations, but, of course' – a pause and a look – 'no need to overdo things. We don't want you cracking up too, now, do we? Physician heal thyself, eh?' A last little laugh to ease his departure but, as he walked off, leaving me standing there, I knew he had smelt the drink on my breath.

Let me draw a veil over the rest of that terrible day when I felt I was at my lowest ebb and, while we're about it, the succeeding ones as well, for a week at least. Sufficient to say, I managed to get through them without anything too terrible happening. I also managed the nights as well, with the help of three, four, sometimes five of the miniatures. Neither colour nor label were considerations any longer. The contents were, and sent me to sleep fast and efficiently. I managed to wake on time when the morning came without the alarm and to arrive looking presentable, and afterwards I managed to get through the rest of the day. I was doing what the patients did: I was *managing*. As I moved about among my fellow sleep-walkers the thought didn't amuse me. If I'd taken off my white coat I could have passed for any one of them.

Duty still took me up to the second floor but when I did go into the recreation room my theory seemed to be holding up. My place, if I still had one, was among the dead ones, certainly not with that lively little group gathered by the window gossiping and laughing around their leader. So I kept my head down and waited for the first patient to come to the trolley for his medication in his own good time.

It was a week before I saw Dr Beck again. Then, one morning, as I was drifting along one of the upper corridors, I looked down and saw him getting out of his little Citröen. Strangely enough, I

51

don't think I'd ever seen him without his white coat before; he looked completely different, more foreign too, because he wore his overcoat in that way, unbuttoned and swinging from the shoulder. He had a hat on as well, moss-green, matching the coat, with a tiny feather in the band. I watched him until he trotted up the steps and disappeared inside. It seemed I had gained some tiny advantage, catching him unawares like that, but later that day it was swept away when Dobbs, grinning as though he knew all my secrets, came up to me and said, 'Beck wants to see you in his office. Who's been a naughty boy, then?'

I spent at least ten minutes in the wash room sprucing myself up, most of that rinsing and gargling, then I went to meet my fate. Outside it was a perfect, still day, I remember, the sort to build up false hopes. Birds had been singing on my way to work – and this in November.

Dr Beck had his windows open and the sound of a distant chainsaw could be heard somewhere deep in the grounds. He sat at his desk writing in a leather-bound ledger and motioned me to sit until he'd finished. I looked at the pictures on his walls. They seemed to be by the same artist and were all female nudes, fat and sprawling, with dark bushy hair in their armpits and elsewhere. I was reminded of the magazine Dobbs had shown me that day in the linen closet.

Dr Beck capped his fountain pen and put his hands together like a little brown Pope.

'It's a sin to be indoors on such a day. Don't you agree? I've taken the liberty, therefore, of planning a nature ramble for three o'clock. You'll find the group waiting for you on the front steps. Two hours in the open should be about ample at this time of year.' He looked at me. 'It should make a pleasant change for you, as well.'

I stood up; there was nothing for me to say and, as well, he had gone back to his writing. I left him there surrounded by his fat naked harem and went to get ready for my open air encounter.

At three o'clock I was on the steps – as I had been ordered: no doubt in my mind on that score. I was wearing the clothes I travel to work in, my proofed jacket, Arran sweater, ordinary trousers with a slight flare – perfectly adequate for what Dr Beck had in mind. Wellingtons would have added the finishing touch but my shoes would just have to do. Anyway, I was determined that I was not going to get involved in anything too strenuous if I could help it. I was wondering what strange get-ups the others might have chosen when suddenly they appeared above me between the pillars of the doorway. They were packed together in a compact bunch and they wore anoraks with the hoods up, even Stella, which surprised me.

I expected them to make their way down to where I was standing waiting, but they hung there until *he*, Gavin, pushed his way through. Ignoring me completely, he strode down the steps, then turned at the bottom to face the others. He had on a sleeveless green jacket, quilted in a diamond pattern, over a navy sweater, brown cords tucked into what looked like ski boots and, on his head, a flat tweed cap and, oh, yes, a tartan scarf to complete the ensemble, in what I imagine were the clan colours. Young Master Gavin Ogilvy presented his back to me, every inch the gentleman, while I hung there feeling foolish.

Stella said, 'Do we *have* to go, Gavin?' but where were those tough tones we had grown used to?

Connie, her face scrubbed and shining, cried out, 'Oh, but it will be marvellous! Really it will, you'll see! Won't it, Gavin?'

Silly, feeble bitch, I thought. But, then, looking at them huddled there in their anoraks like a bunch of middle-aged schoolchildren, I felt sorry for them. What chance had they against this little dictator in his country squire's rig-out? Like the rest of his class he was eager to manipulate people, good at it, as well, from long practice. Even in a place like this the old values

53

still held. It seemed strange that such a thought should take root like that at such a time and in such a place, but it did, and I felt curiously the better for it. The enemy was there with his back to me, not at the top of the steps. Remember that, Kenneth, I told myself.

The enemy said, 'We mustn't allow ourselves to become lazy. Exercise, exercise and, while we're about it, we can also keep our ears and eyes open to what's around us. Can anyone tell me what that species over there is?' He pointed to a dozy looking bird with fluffed-up plumage on top of an ornamental urn. They looked at it with the strain of trying to please written on their faces.

'Crow?' suggested Fergus.

'Lark?' from Connie.

I said, 'It's a thrush,' without thinking.

For the first time they turned their eyes on me, all except *him*, of course, and the hatred there was plain to see.

'Thrush,' I repeated. 'Missel thrush. Songbird. Female.'

Declan giggled. Then Connie came down the steps in a rush. 'Who asked *you*, anyway?'

The others followed and, in a moment, I was left standing there watching them disappear around the corner of the building. The temptation to let them go off on their own was strong, but even though the thought of some mishap happening to them with *him* in charge was attractive, I knew I would be the one to be blamed. I set off after them.

It certainly seemed a strange start to a nature ramble. Back there the way led through a wilderness of dustbins, fire escapes and propped ladders, all those awkward, ugly objects that stay hidden behind the public face of a building. Hanging back, I watched our little dictator leading his straggling band through this obstacle course and, for one marvellous moment, it came to me that perhaps he might have made a miscalculation. But then, no, I told myself, he was much too clever for that. He would have surveyed the ground in advance. I had a sudden image of him high at his window in Willis Wing, spying out the geography of the entire place with a terrible patience, day in, day out, hour after hour, planning for that moment when he would come into his own. As far as I was concerned that time had arrived.

He was taking them deep into the woods, that soon became clear, and I tracked them by the sound of their progress through the trees. There was a great deal of crashing and panting and, as if that wasn't enough to scare off any wild life for miles, Connie and Fergus seemed to be playing some kind of hide and seek as well. Soon I was sweating and my face and hands stung from insect bites. Every step seemed to release them in vicious swarms from their winter quarters, but perhaps it was the unseasonal heat in the air. I suppose that this was what they called an Indian summer, when Nature, humans too, throw off restraint a bit unwisely. A moment later it was as if the theory had come terribly true, for all sounds from the party ahead suddenly ceased. I stopped and listened but heard nothing but my own heavy breathing. The dangers I should have taken into consideration but hadn't came rushing into my head, pitfalls and animal traps, fallen and falling trees, even swamps. There are no quicksands in Ireland, north or south, I told myself, but where was the consolation in that? I began to run, praying I would not be too late.

Now it was my turn to go blundering headlong through that dense growth, heedless of the noise I was making. As I ran I held my outstretched arms before my eyes, ducking oncoming boughs as best I could. Already I hated the place and its luxuriance as much as I hated the one who had forced me into this. He, of course, had been able to choose his own sweet course as well as pace. The sort of unfair treatment fate seemed to be dealing out made me want to weep.

And then I spotted them. They had stopped in a clearing and were gathered about Connie who was kneeling on the fallen leaves. She had something in her hand which she was raising to her mouth.

I yelled, 'No! Don't! Don't!'

They turned to look at me as I ran forward. I dashed the fungus out of her hand.

'Are you fucking mad?' I shouted. I confess I didn't think of what I was saying in the heat of the moment. 'That's a toadstool! They're poison! *Poison!*'

Connie began to cry and the others muttered angrily. 'Go away,' said Lyle.

'Yes, go away,' Harold chipped in.

'*You* used a bad word,' said Fergus.

Stella had a look on her face that said she might well forget her hard-won femininity.

Then Gavin said, 'It's a perfectly harmless *boletus edulis*. Eaten

57

everywhere on the Continent.'

I looked at him as he stood there defying me, hands in pockets, little scarf casually knotted. It wasn't tartan after all, I realised, but a Rupert Bear. At any rate I wanted to throttle him with it and, boy, did he know it.

'You'll find I'm right, if you take the trouble to look it up.'

I stared at the already blackening flesh of the thing on the ground where I had flung it. To me it was still a toadstool. Someone like me from my background made no distinction. He was reminding me of that fact, as well as my ignorance.

Connie said, 'Why do you always have to go and spoil everything?' It was no use my saying, 'Because I'm in charge, that's why,' for it was no longer the truth.

I must have appeared a sorry sight standing there. I didn't need any mirror to convince me of that, I could see it in their faces. That can be the cruellest reflection of all. We were no more than a few paces apart yet the divide between us was as wide as any continent. I felt I might be reduced to sign language for anything I might say would only come out now as foreign babble. My face was hot and stinging; I was bleeding too, and my clothes were thick with burrs. Again I saw all that in their eyes as they turned away and left me there.

After they'd gone I sat down wearily on a tree stump. More of the things were growing out of its decayed wood, the palest and prettiest pink underneath. The more enticing they looked the deadlier they were, everyone knew that. Why should I surrender all my hard-earned lore? More important, why take everything from *him* as holy writ, like the others? Breaking off a piece of the spongy mass, I sniffed; I had no intention of tasting. The smell was faintly peppery. I could imagine a burning sensation on the lips and tongue if someone was foolish or misguided enough to eat. But what if that had been the intention?

And here we come to an awkward thing. I find it difficult to use the word 'evil'. It's such an old-fashioned concept really. Certainly there's no place for it in Dr Beck's scheme of things. We have our fair share of religious obsessives here, more than most, if you care to think about it, and many of those are convinced that Satan actually exists. *He's* been seen regularly in all sorts of places, several times perched on the roof and, once, walking on the lake, now drained, by the woman who went in after him, but that was a classic case of confusion. That sort of thing can be simply and easily explained, but what about the thing itself, *it?* When I was fifteen I had my first real experience. It involved one of the masters at school. Now, Dr Beck would say that a man like that couldn't help himself. Maybe so, but I happen to know that he *enjoyed* it. And now, for the second time in my life, I had come up against someone else who took the same pleasure in evil. And the terrible thing was that I was just as powerless to deal with it now as I had been then. I had learned nothing, nothing . . .

It was very still there in that little glade. I could have been anywhere, in any country, dropped down, as it were, from the heavens, unknown, unwanted. Believe me, you don't have to be drowning to have your life rewind at speed inside your head. It can happen at any time and it was happening to me now. There seemed to be a depressing predictability about it all, like travelling by a circular route past certain recurring landmarks. As I say, there I was, alone, head in hands, staring down at a square foot of leaf-mould – beech, judging by the trees around me – and it was as if my very existence depended on memorising each and every detail of that miniature landscape between my feet.

I don't know how long I stayed like that. It must have been a considerable time, because when I jumped up suddenly my head swam and the trees moved in and out of focus. What made me do that I cannot say to this day, I just knew something was happening and I waited for the message to reach me. Then, again, perhaps I made that up much later, but I do know I was on my feet *59* and certainly listening when the screaming first began. At first I couldn't make out whether it was a man or a woman who was in agony: that sort of pain blurs such distinctions. I strained hard in concentration as if it was important. God forgive me, but I stayed like that, making no move. What must have been going through my head, of course, was a feeling of retribution, always something to be savoured, no matter what the circumstances. They hadn't listened to me, I had tried to warn them of the dangers, but all I had received were insults for my pains. There was no doubt in my mind about who was responsible for the screaming. The sound continued steady and unnatural like a siren that wouldn't stop until someone did something about it, and I knew who that someone had to be. I began to run, then, in the direction of the sound. It must have been about four o'clock; the day was dying fast. Later, the police were to ask about that, the time, I mean, when I found them, but it never struck me to look at my watch.

Once again they were in a glade but not neatly grouped, as that first time. They had each retreated to its outer edge, driven there by what lay huddled on the grass. Which of them can it be, I asked myself, counting, for they were all there. Lyle. I couldn't see Lyle. But first I had to deal with Fergus. He was kneeling with his hands together as though in prayer, but there was nothing spiritual about the noise he was making. I went over to him and slapped him hard – brutally, but medically sound – and the screaming stopped. Connie was moaning quietly, the rest hung or crouched as though in some sort of frozen tableau. *He* had his back to a tree with the same old grin on his face, but looking somewhat forced.

But what had happened to Lyle? I still couldn't bear to go near him. Something in the way he lay there, something dislocated about the arms and legs – I couldn't see his face, it was buried in the hood of his anorak – held me back. Then I noticed his shoes were missing, a sock as well, and the anorak was olive-green, not our regulation blue. Its fabric was punctured and slashed in

60

several places, exposing pale tufts of kapok. Whoever it was, it wasn't Lyle.

'Where's Lyle? *Where is he?*' I shouted, but it was like asking directions from the deaf.

Connie said quite distinctly, 'We must find the other one. It's cold and dark out there. Poor, poor babes in the wood, poor little babes in the wood.'

'Don't worry, we will,' I said, 'we will. There's nothing to be afraid of,' and I meant it. I looked at them scattered around the edge of the clearing. With their hoods pulled up they looked like ancient children, for I was seeing them for what they really were. My eyes had somehow become blinded to the twitches and grimaces, the shaking hands and disjointed gait, always too fast or too slow, the look that comes from chemicals.

In a calm, unhurried voice I said, 'We're going back now, back to a nice hot bath and then it will be time for tea. I'll lead the way and I want Harold to bring up the rear. You'll do that for me, won't you, Harold?' He nodded solemnly. I had chosen him because he looked least put out by the whole business. That could turn out to be a mistake, but I had to take that chance.

They began to line up, well away from the bundle of torn clothing heaped on the grass. No one mentioned Lyle. I looked over to where *he* still stood with his back to the tree. He hadn't moved, nor had that grin, fixed and creepy as a Hallowe'en mask. The others waited, hunched in their anoraks.

I walked over to him. 'Gavin,' I said softly, 'be a good boy, now, and join the others.' Then, even more softly, 'If you don't, I'll have to leave you here. You wouldn't want that to happen, would you, now?' But, of course, I could tell I was talking to stone.

Moving closer, I reached out to straighten his little yellow scarf. 'That's better.' I gave his cheek a pat. Such skin, not a blemish. I looked into his eyes. The pupils were the size of pencil points. There was nothing I could do here, I could tell. I would have to *61*

leave him like that, as though fixed to the living wood at his back, he and whatever horror it was that had returned to haunt him. But none of that was my concern just then. I had other more important responsibilities. They came pressing back. I felt I had recovered from a long illness – that weak but pleasant feeling. Brushing down my clothes, I straightened myself up. My little band was waiting. Back through the perilous woods, huddled in their pixie hoods, I would lead them, back to warmth and safety.

62 A happy ending.

We started off, Harold humming a hymn tune. Then at the last moment, I made the mistake of looking back at the bundle lying on the grass. By some chance of wind or natural settlement a hand had uncovered itself. The colour of ink, the wrist was bound to the other hidden one by electrical flex.

Harold sang, 'Hills of the North rejoice', and my seven dwarfs and I, we turned our backs on the cruel, ugly, outside world. Let it take care of its own mess. I was in charge again.

FIVE

That was over a month ago and everything is back to the way it once was. Once upon a time – as I begin my little stories up on the second floor. A talent, it seems, was lying undiscovered there all along. It's very flattering to have such an attentive audience, not just Fergus and Connie, either, who always loved that sort of thing, but Declan and Harold, George and Lyle, even Stella, but then I've become something of a hero as far as Stella is concerned.

Knitting away prodigiously, she keeps a brotherly eye on me. 'Tell us that one again about you and your mother and Judy Garland's autograph,' and off I start, making it up as I go.

Dr Beck appears very pleased too. It seems he was more than impressed by the way I handled my end of things, particularly when the police came. But I simply told them what I had seen, which was not a lot, in the circumstances. They didn't get too much sense from the others, as far as I can make out, so perhaps my statement appeared vastly superior by comparison. It seemed the corpse was that of a garage hand from the town who had got drunk one night and talked about a car bomb he was supposed to know nothing about. Dobbs told me. Also, that there were twenty-seven stab wounds in the torso, the sort of detail I didn't wish to hear. But, being Dobbs, how could he keep it to himself? I'm sure he didn't count them personally – even Dobbs isn't quite up to that – but he did offer up a vivid and detailed picture of what   *67* he found when he and the other two nurses arrived on the scene.

Their first concern was to find Lyle, then get Gavin back safely but, of course, they had to take a look at the body first – 'strangled, *then* stabbed.' I tried not to dwell on those bound wrists. It isn't any affair of mine, after all, what goes on out there in that world. Let them do their terrible things to one another. At first they were about to beat the woods to find poor Lyle but something about the one standing by the tree made them change their minds. It took three of them, Dobbs said, to move him from the spot and then he had to be manhandled back most of the way. 'Weighed a ton, as if he'd turned to lead, and a grin on his face like it was all a great joke.' Lyle found his own way home and, as far as we can tell, there have been no ill effects. He went straight over to his piano as if nothing had happened.

As for Gavin, well, he's back in Willis Wing indefinitely and none of us has set eyes on him since – well, not until last night. I was on late shift – no, I must be exact, I *arranged* to be on late shift. I swapped with one of the night nurses, something I've never done before, but I wanted to do what I had to do in my own way and in my own time. I had thought about it a lot since that day in the woods. Dr Beck's first words had been, 'I'm afraid we've lost him,' when he saw the state of his prize patient that day, but I had to satisfy myself that never again would I come through a door and suffer that destructive grin from the far side of the room.

Believe me when I say there was never at any time a thought of gloating or revenge in mind. Certainly I had some right – I had suffered because of him – but it's not in my nature. I leave that to people like Dobbs and his ilk. No, it was a matter of simply seeing for myself, of closing an episode. And so here I was about to do that very thing in the only way I could think of . . .

At three in the morning the world is a very different place, as well as everyone in it. Padding about on rubber soles along the corridors under the half lights, I felt like the last man alive.

Perhaps the feeling suited me. I needed more time to find out. In No 4 Ward I tiptoed past beds, watching, listening. I saw Stella's head on the pillow in curlers, Harold's teeth in a glass, Declan's hands lying still on the covers as innocent as a choirboy's. They slept like children washed clean of cares.

Leaving them to their dreams I passed on my way and never had I such strong feelings of affection towards each and every one of them. Looking back down that row of white painted beds, no matter what, I told myself, would I ever betray that trust. Or let anything or anyone, for that matter, interfere with it in any way.

To satisfy some whim, I know not what, I unlocked the door to the recreation room and looked in. Moonlight from the far windows threw a wide bright path across to where I stood. The chairs sat empty, just as their occupants had left them, and on the low tables games of draughts waited to be resumed. I don't think I had ever seen it like this before, but then how many of us had? I felt the guardian of something, my own little kingdom, perhaps, for what it was worth. Tomorrow I planned to introduce a new game to the group. It still hadn't quite suggested itself but something much more demanding seemed to be called for. The time had come to put aside childish things for all of us.

I closed the door, locked it, and continued on my nocturnal travels. It was like visiting a new country where no one had ventured before.

On the upper corridor now I looked down at the grounds, dark and wooded far below. My mind floated free. I fancied I was on a liner – no, a dimly-lit aircraft passing low and slow over those same treetops. Approaching came a break in the timber, a clearing of some kind. It looked magical, untouched, a secret rendezvous for wild things but then, something not quite right, glimpsed quickly, that shadowy heap on the grass, and surely that must be human movement there by the largest tree. Another glade comes sliding into view now: this one looks man-made and, indeed, there is a structure of some sort down there, its metallic roof catching the light. It seems familiar, somehow. There's a shirt pegged to an invisible line, a bicycle, an empty gas cylinder awaiting collection . . .

Afterwards it came to me just how little real distance separated those two places on the map, but at the time I didn't tell the police about my night visitors. There may have been a connection, but again I don't wish to think about that. All I know is there's been nothing of the sort since. Anyway, I've made up my mind to sell the mobile home. Dr Beck says he can find a flat for me here in the hospital. It's a chapter that's closed, as far as I'm concerned, except for this one last thing that I had to do.

As I say, in the small hours the world is a different place, but up here it's always been like that. The lights are always softer, as is the flooring underfoot, and there's a pleasant scent to the air, nothing like that of the public wards I'd just come from. Spring-like. All that was missing was piped music.

I seemed to be floating along past those locked doors on cushioned feet and at the same time I was feeling highly-charged. It may well have been the pill I had swallowed earlier, but then again perhaps something deeper had a hand in it.

His number was forty-two, yes, just like in an hotel, and I stopped outside the door. No peepholes up here on Willis Wing. I listened for a moment, then took out the bunch of keys I had brought with me from the orderly room. The action of the lock was as silent as I could wish for, and I held the handle a second before carefully pressing inwards. There was a dim night-light somewhere in the room and I held myself in the doorway until I could see better. The bed and its occupant were shadowy, but the rest of the room gradually asserted itself. It was not as I'd imagined. If it had once been luxurious or even moderately comfortable, now it had been stripped bare of everything except a bed; no carpet, no pictures, no curtains, even the window glass

70

had been painted with that white stuff that workmen use to keep out prying eyes. The only light came from a dim bulb high on a side wall in a wire security basket. It reminded me of the old refractory ward, no longer in use now that a single injection can do the work of a thousand yards of webbing and canvas. I had seen the effect of the needle on the most violent of cases, and could well imagine the state of the man in the bed. His breathing continued slow and steady but I still could make out nothing but a shape beneath the sheets. I came further into the room. There was a faint smell of vomit. With my hand on the chill bed-rail I stood there listening and, God knows, there was no need to linger longer. If further proof were needed that the case was closed where was it to come from? But something was still eating away at me. This thing, whatever it was, made me move closer to the shadowed head until I felt breath on the back of my hand. I brought my face down to the hidden one.

'It's me,' I whisper. 'Kenny. Remember Kenny? He did try to warn you, you know, and now look at the state you've got yourself into. That day in the woods brought it all back. It did, didn't it? That *thing* lying there. But you would insist on going in there without Kenny. That was silly of you. I hope you see that now. Don't think about it any more. It'll pass like a bad dream. Believe me, I know, I've had my own share of setbacks. I know you don't want to be reminded about it but – that girl – the one who got you into this mess – she probably deserved everything she got. I know what girls like that can be like. I know the type. If you'd had Kenny for a friend then, it might never have happened. But it's not too late, we can still be friends. Call me Kenny, if you like. We can start all over again . . .'